This edition published by Parragon Books Ltd in 2014

Parragon Books Ltd
Chartist House
15–17 Trim Street
Bath BA1 1HA, UK
www.parragon.com

ISBN 978-1-4723-9053-0

Printed in Poland

STORIES FROM ARENDELLE

Bath • New York • Cologne • Melbourne • Delhi
Hong Kong • Shenzhen • Singapore • Amsterdam

ANNA

Princess Anna is smart,
loving and kind.
She adores her big sister,
Elsa, and wants to
spend time with her.
When Elsa gets into
trouble, Anna leaps into
action. She is very brave
and is always looking for
a new adventure!

ELSA

Queen Elsa might seem cold
and uncaring, but it's only
because she has a secret – she
has the power to control ice
and snow! Elsa needs to
be careful and controlled
because she wants to protect
her little sister, Anna,
and the people
of her kingdom.

Kristoff & Sven

Kristoff is the strong and silent type, but he likes to spend time with Anna and his loyal reindeer friend, Sven. Kristoff works hard on his ice business and knows how to survive in the cold mountains.

OLAF

Olaf is a funny, loving and trusting
snowman created by Queen Elsa.
He's very curious and really wants
to be helpful. Olaf's biggest wish
is to see summer – he doesn't
understand that he would
melt under the
hot sun!

From the movie
Disney
FROZEN

PHANTOMS OF ARENDELLE

Written by Landy Quinn Walker

PROLOGUE

Anna was holding a ghost! She and her sister, Elsa, had been tracking the phantom for hours, following it through the secret passageways hidden inside Arendelle's castle walls. Then Elsa had created a giant ice slide to catch up with the phantom … and it had worked! Unfortunately, Anna, Elsa and the captured spirit were now rocketing down the slippery ice slide – with no way to stop.

This was not how Anna had expected to spend her day. Right then she was supposed to be throwing a massive ball in Elsa's honour. She had been planning it for days, right under Elsa's nose. Streamers and cake and chocolates and musicians and everything! It had taken all Anna's efforts to keep her sister distracted, out of the castle, and away from her duties as Queen of Arendelle during the set-up. And now they were trapped in these hidden hallways and would miss the dance anyway!

Ahead, Anna could see that the passage was coming to a dead end. The sisters and the phantom shot towards the bottom of the slide, and Elsa created a huge snowbank to stop them before they hit the oncoming castle wall. Anna considered the snowbank and the wall behind it. "It'll be just like a pillow," she reminded herself. But that wall looked very solid – and it was coming up fast.

Only one thing was certain: what had started as a simple plan for a surprise dance had become something much crazier.

CHAPTER 1

It was the previous morning and Anna was trying to think of a plan.

The young princess flipped another page of the gigantic library book she had pulled off the shelf – a book of myths and legends from around the world. It was one of her favourites from when she was little, when her sister, Elsa, had still been hiding from the world. Back then, Anna had worked her way through nearly every book in the library. There hadn't been much else to do.

Now things were very different. Everything about life in the castle had changed since Elsa had returned home from the North Mountain and learned to control her powers. By Elsa's royal decree, the gates were always open, sunlight streamed through the unshuttered windows and villagers and guests came and went freely every day. There were so many new people to meet: blacksmiths and glassblowers and cheesemongers. There was even a man whose entire job was to repair dolls' shoes. He was a doll cobbler and his work was amazing! Everything was great....

But Anna sometimes found herself thinking about all the things her sister had missed out on while she was locked away: birthday celebrations and playing with friends and everything. All of them had drifted by. Life had been lonely for Anna, but for Elsa it had been so much more difficult. And Anna knew how much happier her sister was now. But on days like this, when Elsa was especially busy with her duties as queen, Anna couldn't help wondering if she could make Elsa's life even better.

So there she was, sitting in the library, pondering

what to do. What would be a great way to properly welcome her sister back to a world of open doors?

Anna turned another page of the book. This story was about a gigantic spell-casting octopus monster. What kind of spells a gigantic octopus monster would cast wasn't clear. It didn't matter. She always skipped ahead so she could read her favourite section – the tale of a giant boar that could transform into shadow. He guided his princess bravely through the land of giants, keeping her safe from discovery by her enemies. When she was six, Anna had decided the heroic boar should be named Spy Pig.

"Anna!" a happy voice called out from nearby. "I'm so glad to see you! I've missed you so much!"

Anna turned, a small smile forming on her lips. "I saw you this morning, Olaf!" she responded to the little snowman as he walked into the library. "At breakfast, remember? Just before Kristoff and Sven left on their ice delivery?"

Olaf climbed into a chair near Anna, the snowflakes from his personal snow cloud tickling her arm. "Really? It feels like such a long time ago! I've spent all morning looking at books! Did you know that every one of these books is completely different?"

"Yeah!" Anna laughed. "I've read most of these already … a lot of them twice, actually." Anna pointed at the book Olaf had brought in with him. "So … uh … what do you have there?"

Olaf lit up with excitement. "A book about phantoms!" he exclaimed. "Did you know they are everywhere? Especially in castles like … well, like this one! Gerda has been reading it to me! Do you know her?"

Anna nodded with amusement. "Only my whole life! Gerda and Kai have been overseeing the castle household since before I was born." Anna poked at the book Olaf was holding. "But I think that if there were any ghosts or phantoms or whatever here, I would know. I *am* the princess, after all. I think all ghosts have to report to me by law or something."

Olaf was less amused. "You shouldn't laugh about these things, Anna. It says so right here. See?"

Olaf held up his book. The title was *Do Not Laugh at Phantoms!*

Olaf continued. "From what Gerda read to me, phantoms are invisible and they can't talk to anyone unless that person talks to them first. And even then they have to be reminded of what their mortal life was before they became spirits. Don't you see? It's lonely and hard being a ghost. Everything drifts by them and no one ever talks to them or asks them to play or sing or dance…. They need our help so they can remember how to enjoy themselves. They need –"

"Whoa," Anna said, interrupting the small snowman. "Olaf, you're so right. You're so totally right about everything!"

Olaf looked awestruck. "I knew it! I knew the phantoms were real!"

But Anna was already running out of the library. She would make sure that Elsa never again felt like things were drifting by her and she knew just how to do it. She had a great plan – the best of plans.

But, first, she would need a pig.

CHAPTER 2

Elsa picked up the next sheet from the huge pile of paperwork on her desk and tried to focus on it.

"Annual report on projected dandelion pollination … reservation committee … subparagraph three … all rights withstanding…."

With a thunk, the newish Queen of Arendelle let her head fall on to her desk. She let out a sleepy yawn, even though it was barely midday. Normally she wouldn't be this tired, paperwork or no paperwork. But she had been up late the night before, working out the details of the surprise banquet for her younger sister, Anna.

Elsa had been planning it with her court counsellors for weeks and now it was just one day away. It was a complicated event and everything had to go just right … which especially meant that Anna couldn't know about it. If she found out … well, then it wouldn't be much of a surprise, would it?

Elsa returned her attention to the paper in her hand. But before she could begin to read it, a loud squeal distracted her. It sounded almost like a …

"Pig!" Anna's voice rose over the squealing. "No, seriously! *Pig!*"

Elsa looked up and immediately saw why Anna was yelling "pig." It was because there was a little pink pig running into the room and clambering up on to the desk.

"What the…? Why…?" was all Elsa could stammer before the pig crashed across her desk, scattering everything she had been working on.

Anna leaped across the room, attempting to tackle the frantic animal. "I told you, 'pig'!" she yelled as the wriggling creature evaded her grasp. "That was because … you know … *pig*!"

Elsa waved a hand. The temperature instantly dropped. A sparkling shimmer appeared around the suddenly confused animal and formed into an icy fence.

Anna looked impressed by her sister's quick reflexes. "Aw, who's a cute little guy?" she said, reaching into the frozen pigpen and scratching the pig's fuzzy head.

The pig cocked his head and let out a tiny squeal of happiness.

"'Cute little guy'?" Elsa looked around the wreckage of her office. "That pig just destroyed …" She stopped and shook her head, realizing she wasn't asking the most important question. "Wait … why is there a pig in the castle?"

Anna lit up at the question. "Okay … call me crazy, but I had this idea! There's a story in the library … the one about the boar that can transform into shadows? What if we made this cute little guy into that boar?"

Elsa held up her hands to slow Anna down. "I remember the story, but this … this …" She looked at the round pink pig. It looked back at her. "This isn't a boar. It's a pig."

Anna scratched the happy pig's nose. It oinked at her in a friendly way. "But we could teach him to be a mighty shadow boar!" She grabbed the pig gently by its cheeks and made happy faces at it through the icy pen. "Yes, we could, Spy Pig! Yes, we could!"

"Anna …"

Anna finally seemed to notice Elsa's sceptical look. "Okay …" Anna continued. "You're not loving the Spy Pig plan. I can sense that. Still –"

Before Anna could say any more, the pig flexed its legs and leaped over the top of the pigpen, then ran out of the door with a joyful squeal.

"Spy Pig! Come back!" Anna yelled, dashing down the hallway after it.

Elsa hesitated for a moment. She could stay there and review the expected revenue of the outlying farms … or she could run after Anna and help train a pig to be a mythical shadow beast.

Then she realized that this distraction might just be exactly what she needed. If she could keep Anna busy, then the castle staff could make the preparations for Anna's surprise banquet without any possible interruption. It was too good an opportunity to pass up.

And so she didn't.

CHAPTER 3

The Spy Pig plan had been a huge success.

Anna and Elsa were lying in matching collapsed heaps on a grassy patch of the royal gardens. They were covered in an absurd amount of mud and Anna was pretty sure even her bruises had bruises. And Spy Pig had long since fled, disappearing back towards the castle and abandoning his very important spy missions.

But it had been great fun *and* an entire afternoon's diversion and that was what mattered. Anna's plan to share all kinds of new things with Elsa was well on its way. So many fun experiences that everyone should enjoy with someone they loved, all crammed into two days, culminating on the second night in the most fantastic ball Arendelle had ever seen!

And that was where the diversion came in. Anna wanted the ball to be a surprise and secret dances took a lot of preparation. To that end, Anna had managed to get Elsa outside for an entire afternoon so the castle staff could make plans, prepare the music and guest list, order the banners and special dessert – and then hide everything away. Then, when Elsa returned to the castle, she would be none the wiser.

But Anna couldn't let Elsa know that she was purposefully being kept from the castle. There was still so much to do!

"Okay," Anna said, "maybe Spy Pig wasn't the sneakiest of spies. Maybe …"

Elsa responded with a groan. "'Maybe'? It was seen by everyone in the entire village! It would have been more spy-like if it had been singing and dancing through the square! Despite our best efforts, I don't think that pig is destined to be a shadow boar."

"I think you're probably right," Anna said, getting to her feet. "So what do we do now?"

Elsa hesitated. "Now?"

"There's so much more for us to do!" Anna exclaimed. "So many games and adventures and all sorts of things. Let's not stop now!" She grabbed her sister's hands eagerly. "Think about all the things you ever wanted to do! With me! Together! We could learn to duel, practise skipping, attend a carnival, eat triple-double-fudge sundaes ..."

Elsa looked up at her sister with a serious expression. "I was hiding in my room. I wasn't dead. I ate many a triple-double-fudge sundae."

Anna smiled. "But not with me!"

Elsa paused for thought. She looked as if maybe she wanted to argue against Anna's impeccable logic. But then she sighed and Anna knew she had her sister convinced.

"Okay … okay," Elsa said with a small laugh. "It's a lot to do. So, I guess we'd better get started."

CHAPTER 4

The sisters ran around the village for the rest of the evening. By the end they were both exhausted from their adventures and decided to spend the night in the most comfortable bed in the nicest inn in town – which was great, since a sleepover in a new place was one of the things Anna had suggested that they should experience.

In the morning, they picked up right where they had left off. By the time they had lunch and were rocking together on the porch swing outside the inn, Elsa could barely remember everything she and Anna had managed to do. There had been a race on horseback, an archery competition, the sampling of every kind of cheese she had ever heard of (and several she hadn't) and three puppet shows that Anna had performed with reluctant help from Kai and Gerda.

And it had been great. Elsa had really enjoyed trying all kinds of new things with her sister. Unfortunately, she could see that Anna was getting tired, sinking back into the cushions as they rocked. But it was the day of the banquet and Elsa knew the staff was, at that very moment, setting up the Great Hall. If Anna went back to the castle and wandered anywhere near there, she was bound to see something that would give away the surprise.

"You can't quit now!" Elsa said with mock gravity in her voice. "We've barely done half of the things you've been saying we should do!"

Anna looked surprised. But then she sat up, scrunched up her face and rubbed her hands together excitedly. "All right, then," Anna said. "You pick. What's next?"

Elsa looked at her sister and replied in a solemn voice, "Pillow fight."

And with that, she jumped up, grabbed a cushion off the swing and delivered the first blow. Anna recovered quickly, snatching a cushion to defend herself with.

With a squeal of laughter, the battle began.

CHAPTER 5

Meanwhile....

Olaf knocked on the castle walls. From what he could tell, there was almost certainly some kind of haunting going on in the castle. First off, people kept whispering about a mysterious-sounding pig that had run through the hallways and was never seen again. That certainly wasn't the normal sort of thing that one would expect in a nice castle, so it had to be phantom-related. Olaf had also heard people talking about a small pale creature that walked the castle freely, leaving gusts of cold wind in his wake. And no one spoke of this strange being with fear, which told Olaf that it wasn't just well known – it was friendly, too!

According to *Do Not Laugh at Phantoms!*, this was absolute proof of a Class-Three Haunting – a happy and welcoming spirit that's too shy to say hello. Olaf couldn't wait to meet it!

He knocked on another wall, this one sporting a large mirror, and listened intently for any response. There was no answering sound … but the mirror slowly opened, like a door. Like a *secret* door. Olaf smiled. This had to be where the phantoms were hiding!

And with that, he stepped into the secret passageway, almost – but not quite – closing the mirrored door behind him.

CHAPTER 6

After the pillow battle, Anna had convinced Elsa to go out to the fjord and use her ice powers to make sculptures on the surface of the water. Each one was an amazing work of art, made all the more beautiful by how quickly it melted in the warm summer ocean. And the sisters spending time together at the fjord was especially perfect, as Anna knew that the masterpiece of all the celebratory desserts she had ordered, a gigantic tiered cake, would be arriving at the castle at any minute. Anna just needed to keep Elsa away for a little while longer, while the cake was delivered and the Great Hall was decorated. Then, at nightfall, she could lead her sister to the dance and surprise her with cake and decorations and music and laughter. It would be the perfect end to this perfect couple of days.

The problem was that Elsa had just received an important document from a court messenger and was rushing through the village and back towards the castle entrance.

"Elsa! Wait!" Anna called after her sister. Elsa turned just as twelve strong men carrying what must have been the world's largest cake slowly emerged round the corner of a nearby building.

"Anna," Elsa responded, "this is important –"

Anna practically defied the laws of gravity, leaping to where her sister was standing and turning her by the shoulders just as a parade of streamer-wielding event planners followed the cake-carrying men into view.

"But we have to hurry and *go* …" Anna emphasized as she looked past Elsa and tried to signal the cake and streamer people, "somewhere *else*! A place … where things …" Anna tried desperately to think of something she could say that would stop her sister from turning and seeing the massive cake and the streamers ... as well as the troupe of musicians, who had decided that it was a great time to step outside and take in the air of Arendelle.

Elsa started to turn. Anna did the only thing she could think of. "Look out!" she yelled, pointing into the sky. "Octopus monster!"

Elsa looked up. "What? How ...? Anna ... what are you yelling about? There's no 'octopus monster' in the sky."

The last of the party people had seemed to take the hint and retreated out of sight. Anna breathed a huge sigh of relief.

"Right," she said as Elsa looked at her as if she were the craziest of crazy people. "Good thing you were here to scare it off. Whoo ..."

Elsa shook her head and turned back towards the castle.

It was going to be a long afternoon before the ball finally happened, Anna thought.

CHAPTER 7

It was going to be a long afternoon before the banquet finally happened, Elsa thought as she hurried back into the castle, rereading the note that had been delivered by the court messenger.

She had known she wasn't paying enough attention to the planning of this event. But Anna had been so eager to spend time with her and they had been having so much fun *and* it was keeping her sister occupied while the event arrangements were all finalized.

Unfortunately, in her absence it seemed that everything that could go wrong had gone wrong.

The bakers had run out of ingredients while taking care of some other high-priority special order, the custom-made streamers she had ordered had somehow been mistakenly sold for some other event and the musicians she had booked were no longer available.

She was the queen! What other event could possibly be happening that could get in the way of a surprise dinner for her sister? Not that it mattered right then. What was most important was that she attended to these issues while finding a way to keep her sister occupied. Which would be difficult, as Anna was following her closely every step of the way.

"Anna …" Elsa began gently, taking a hasty route down a side hallway into a more remote wing of the castle to avoid the Great Hall and anyone involved in preparing for the banquet. "Maybe … maybe you should get some rest. You know, you've been running all over and I know you've not been getting a lot of sleep."

Anna waved away the comment. "Pssh.

I'm fine! I get plenty of – wait. Why do you think I need sleep? Do I look tired?"

Anna turned and looked in a mirror hanging on the wall. "Seriously?" she continued. "I mean … a nap would be great and all, but I don't think I – Hey! Look!"

Anna gently pushed on the mirror. It was … open! "It's a secret passage! Inside the castle! Did you know this was here?"

Elsa stepped closer, examining the mirror. It was brilliantly built. Once it closed, you would never know it could open. But who had opened it?

"I had heard rumours, but…." Elsa admitted. "When we were really little kids, Gerda used to tell stories, remember? She said the castle was full of twisty hallways and secret rooms all inside the walls. I never believed her, though."

Anna pushed the door open wider. Inside, it was dark – though not perfectly dark. Just dark enough to be kind of creepy.

"Why didn't you believe her?" Anna asked, exploring the gloomy passageway with her eyes.

The space inside the wall was narrow and cramped but very tall, and it had slim openings – slits in the stone that could have been windows once – way up high that led to the outside world. From these, small amounts of sunlight and air filtered in. Instead of making the passage less creepy, the dim light just highlighted how cramped and uncomfortable-looking it really was.

Elsa shrugged. "I don't know. I guess because she also said the hidden parts of the castle were haunted by spooky ghosts. So I figured the whole thing was just a story to …"

Elsa trailed off as she heard a noise from further up the hallway. Rounding a corner, struggling with an impossibly large cake, were twelve very strong men. The cake…. The bakers must have been mistaken. But if Anna saw it now, the surprise of the great banquet would be ruined.

Without thinking, Elsa shoved Anna inside the dusty passage and pulled the mirror almost completely closed behind her.

"Wha–?" Anna yelped, startled.

Elsa tried to distract her sister. "Oh! Sorry! I, um … I tripped. Over … something … in front of my feet. It…. You know how it goes."

In the dimness, Anna eyed her sister as she moved to the hidden door. "Ohhhh-kay. We'll both pretend you're not being really weird … even for you."

Just then, there was a loud thump and the door shut all the way. The girls shared a look of alarm at the sound of a heavy latch clicking into place.

"What happened?" Anna shouted as she pressed against the spot in the stone wall where the door had been. "No one is ever in those hallways! Who could have closed it?"

The door wasn't opening. That much was clear. But her sister needed an answer and Elsa couldn't tell her it was the cake-carrying men who had bumped into the door, pressing it closed.

She had an idea. She knew Anna wouldn't take it seriously, but it was a fun enough idea that it would distract Anna from asking any more questions about what was happening in the hallway.

So with all the seriousness she could muster, she turned to her little sister and whispered one little word.

"Ghosts."

CHAPTER 8

Olaf was amazed.

The passageways had been dark and there seemed to be no end to them. It was like there was a second castle built inside the walls of the first castle. He had found old storage rooms full of paintings, crates of books and dozens and dozens of chairs and mirrors.

But no phantoms. Not yet, anyway.

As he explored, he found several more secret doorways and passages, eventually leading him out of the walls and into a sealed area of the castle. He had heard that some older sections of the castle had fallen into disuse and been sealed off, but he never thought he'd be lucky enough to see one!

It was here that Olaf had discovered an old dining room.

The dining room seemed really nice. Dusty paintings of kings from a long time ago hung on the walls. Cloths covered all the furniture. The windows had all been bricked over – though a bit of light was filtering through the small cracks between bricks – and only two of the doors led anywhere. One led back the way Olaf had come: a secret passage so filled with boxes that Olaf had barely managed to squeeze through a space at the bottom – and even that had resulted in his body briefly falling into pieces. The other opened into a shadowy hallway that led further into the sealed-off section of the castle.

It was so very interesting! But still he hadn't found any phantoms! Olaf was disappointed.

"Hello? Any ghosts in here? Phantoms or spirits?" Olaf called. "It's okay to come out and be friends now!"

Nothing. But Olaf wasn't one to give up. Everyone needed someone, especially lonely ghosts who lived inside castle walls. But it was difficult, he imagined. After living for so long, lonely in the dark, it would be hard to come out and make a new friend.

So in an effort to make the spirits comfortable, Olaf decided to make the place more inviting.

First he pulled the dust sheet off the table. Then he arranged the dishes that were sitting on it as if he and the ghosts were going to have a nice happy dinner together. He even found a bowl of wax fruit and bottles of juice of some kind to add to the table setting. And with that, he sat down to his pretend meal and began pretend-eating.

"Mmm," Olaf said, "this wax fruit is delicious. If only there were some spirits out there that wanted to join me!"

Then he waited.

And waited.

"Oh, wow," he said, trying again, "and this juice is so refreshing and good…. But it would be so much better if I had someone to share it with!"

No answer. Olaf shrugged. According to what Gerda had read to him from *Do Not Laugh at Phantoms!*, it would take some time to make a ghost feel comfortable enough to show itself. In the meantime, maybe there was more stuff in the hidden hallways that would help.

With that, Olaf hopped off the large wooden chair and wandered away from the dining room. There was so much more to explore!

CHAPTER 9

"These hallways go on forever!" Anna exclaimed.

Elsa followed her sister, listening.

"I mean, it's almost like a new castle was built around an older castle. But that would have had to happen hundreds of years ago!"

"It's amazing," Elsa agreed, pushing against a wall with all her might. "Maybe we can explore it all … tomorrow."

"Well, sure!" Anna said cheerily. "As big as this place seems to be, we could spend all week exploring and still not see it all!"

Elsa grew frustrated. "We don't have all week! We don't have all night! I have important things to plan!"

"Hey! You're not the only one! I have … things, too!"

"Anna …" Elsa started, but then she asked, "Wait, what do you have to plan?"

"Stuff!" Anna said defensively. "Lots of stuff! I mean, I don't have to be a queen to have important plans to plan, do I?"

"That's not what I meant!" Elsa said. "I just mean … the things I'm working on –"

"Doesn't matter! You're taking tonight off!" Anna responded.

"But," replied Elsa, "I have to take care of things! I really do!"

"Not tonight!" Anna pointed at her older sister. "Tonight you are relaxing!"

Elsa looked around at the gloomy passage. "How … how is this relaxing?"

Anna shrugged. "Oh, come on. It's not like we're trapped in here. You have powers!"

Elsa poked the wall, freezing just a tiny section.

"You know that my powers don't open doors! I'd just break down the wall! And I'd really prefer not to wreck the castle if I don't have to."

"Well, yeah … but …" Anna pushed against the wall. Nothing. "I guess that's a fair point … but what else can we do?"

Elsa looked around. "Listen, if I have to, I can get us out. But let's save that for a last resort. There was a doorway in; it stands to reason there must be a doorway out. We can take a little time and explore. Okay?"

Anna looked uncertain. "Okay … for a little while, I guess. But I have serious plans for tonight! We … I can't miss them, so –" Then she stopped short, looking at the dusty floor of the hallway. "Wait. Are these … tiny footprints? They're hard to see, but … they don't … they don't look human…."

Elsa was about to respond when she heard a sound. It came from far away, and it was soft as a whisper. But still … it was unmistakable.

"Was that…?" Anna asked in a hushed voice. "Was that … laughter?"

CHAPTER 10

Olaf laughed with glee. He had a new idea that he thought was sure to work! In a storage room inside the castle walls, he had found racks and crates of old clothes: dresses, suits and uniforms. According to what he had learned, ghosts usually wandered around draped in sheets. They were sure to be less shy if they had fancy clothes instead! So Olaf had unpacked some outfits and laid them out to show them off.

Nothing happened. The clothes just sat there all nicely arranged. Olaf sighed. The snowman was trying everything he could think of. He had even locked a door after he passed through it, to make sure that the spirits didn't drift past him.

He didn't want to miss meeting his future friends! But still … nothing.

"Huh," Olaf said to himself. "Maybe the ghosts prefer the sheets after all…. Ooh! Maybe I had it backwards! Maybe *I* should dress up as a *ghost*!" With that, he grabbed a large moth-eaten sheet and covered himself with it, peering out through the holes that the very considerate moths had made. Then the snowman waddled out of the storage room and up a long flight of wooden stairs.

CHAPTER 11

Anna ran through the narrow and gloomy hallways, her sister trailing behind. The passages were haphazardly arranged, some clearly having been leftover space between walls and others having been purposefully built. They turned and widened and narrowed again unpredictably.

"Anna, wait!" Elsa shouted. "You don't know where you're going!"

Anna kept running, jumping over the occasional crate and ducking under the low beams, yelling back as best she could. "I heard someone! That means we're not alone! Which means maybe they know the – *OOOF!*"

"Oh, no! Anna! Are you okay?"

As Anna rounded a corner, she had run face-first into a large pile of crates and crumpled to the ground.

Anna sat up, looking a bit woozy. "I'm good. I'm okay. Just ... whoo ... just gonna sit for a second...."

In the dim light, Anna looked up at the crates. They were filled with mildewed old uniforms. Clearly they had been tucked away by the castle staff years earlier and completely forgotten by everyone. They were stacked almost to the ceiling of the passageway – and in this small section that meant really, really high.

"Wow ... that's a lot of boxes. Elsa, it's a dead end. Where are we supposed to go now?" Anna asked her sister, not really expecting an answer.

Elsa paused, peering at the ground next to Anna. "Look ... more of those little footprints ..."

Anna leaned over and examined the prints.

They were faint, but visible. "What could have made them?"

Elsa looked around. "I don't know … but we should keep moving."

"Fair enough," Anna agreed. "How will we get past these boxes? It will take hours for us to move them all!"

Elsa didn't respond. Instead, she just waved her hand and a staircase of ice appeared, leading up the tower of crates.

"Or you could just make an ice staircase," Anna said as she stood up. "That would be a good Plan B."

And with that, Anna carefully headed up the slippery stairs, her sister right behind her.

CHAPTER 12

"Okay … this is creepy," Anna whispered.

Anna wasn't wrong, Elsa thought as she surveyed the old dining room.

The sisters had descended the ice staircase and followed more of the strange footprints along a twisty hallway to find that the only way forward was through a crawl space. By the time they had emerged on the other side, both girls were covered in dust. From there, they had found another secret door, which at first they thought was the way out. Instead, the door led to an abandoned section of the castle – closed off for dozens of years by the look of it – and the old dining room they were in.

It was small by Arendelle's current standards and the dusty drapes covering everything gave it a sinister look. Paintings of kings that ruled centuries earlier adorned the walls, with only the slightest cracks in the bricked-over windows allowing any light in. Anna dug through some dirty-looking boxes and found a lantern that still had some oil in it, but the flickering light of the lantern only made the room look spookier. Especially since it allowed the sisters to better see the fully set table, complete with wax food and glasses filled with a sour-looking liquid – a pickling brine of some kind.

"Someone was just here," Elsa noted, pointing out the drops of moisture on the table settings and the freshly polished wax fruit. "Someone just set this table up. But who? And why?"

Anna shook her head. "Maybe the right question is *what* would do this rather than *who*. You said you heard that ghosts live in the castle walls...."

"Anna, those were just stories," Elsa countered. "Old spooky stories that people tell to children!"

"Yeah," Anna said as she sniffed the sour liquid in the wine glass. "Except that someone or some*thing* poured this brine in these glasses and put this wax fruit on the table. Something else is here – inside the castle walls but obviously hiding from us. Why?"

It was Elsa's turn to shake her head. "I don't know! But it can't be a phantom! Ghosts aren't real!"

"I know, I know. It's just …" Anna said, considering the possibilities. "Whatever did move all this around, it had to go somewhere…."

Anna held the lantern up, lighting the door at the other end of the room. Both sisters saw more of the strange footprints leading out of the door. Anna pointed. "That's the only other way out."

"Great!" Elsa said as she moved to the open doorway. "Then let's go prove there are no phantoms and get out of these old rooms!"

CHAPTER 13

Anna shivered. The longer they spent in these passageways, the creepier things got.

With only the light of the lantern to guide them, Anna and Elsa had made their way out of the old dining room. Unfortunately, the sisters couldn't find any direct access from the sealed part of the castle back into the main section or to the outside world.

On the upside, Anna noticed the flame of the lamp flickering in a specific direction, which indicated air moving through the walls. This led the sisters to another partially open secret door, which led to a different secret passageway. Other than being dustier, it was no different from the first one: super-high ceilings, exposed beams, narrow windows letting in small amounts of light.

The sisters moved as quickly as they could, but Anna was getting increasingly concerned about time. The ball was scheduled to start soon and if she missed this … if Elsa missed this….

But there was only so much rushing they could do. Sometimes the space was so narrow they had to scoot through it sideways while holding their breath. Other times the ceiling was so low they practically had to crawl. One stretch of crawlspace was rotting and Elsa had to create a narrow ice bridge for the sisters to get safely across. Another section was blocked by a locked door, which, fortunately, Anna was able to open with a bent hairpin.

The sisters felt like they had been walking for miles, and given how much the passages twisted and turned and doubled back on themselves, they probably had.

And then, suddenly, they found themselves in an old storage room. Along the walls, there were racks and boxes of clothes – mostly old dresses out of fashion for more than a generation and covered in a thick layer of dust.

Mostly.

"Those clothes …" Elsa's voice was quiet. "They've been arranged, like …"

Anna finished the thought. "Like they were being worn by people and the people just vanished?"

It was true. In the centre of the crowded space, a group of ornate outfits lay puddled as if people had been dancing inside them. Near the bottom, shoes could be seen. Unlike the clothes still hanging or folded away, these were relatively dust-free – as if they had been moved very recently.

"But … they must have been like this for years." Elsa answered, "I mean, for whatever reason, they were stored this way. Or …"

Anna poked at a dress, feeling the cloth. Her hand recoiled instantly. "It's cold. Almost as cold as ice."

Elsa grabbed the dress. "It's like it was sitting outside during a winter night! I don't understand. How could it be so cold?"

Anna gestured wildly. "Have you not been listening to anything we've been talking about for the last few hours? Ghosts!"

CHAPTER 14

Olaf travelled a long way up the wooden stairs before he reached a small stone landing protruding from the wall. He was up really high now – probably the highest he could get. Ahead of him, a second set of stairs led back down. "Wow," he said, looking over the edge at the massive drop.

Wow. Wow. Wow. Wow. His voice echoed back.

Olaf considered. He was standing in the perfect place to get the attention of any hidden phantoms. He smiled and took a deep breath.

CHAPTER 15

Anna threw up her hands. "Why did we have to find all this *today*? Here we are, on an adventure through secret passageways following a phantom and we don't have the time to properly enjoy it at all! I mean, *look* at this!" She crouched down next to one of the uniforms, feeling the cold cloth.

Elsa sat down beside her sister. "Anna … we have all the time we need. These passageways aren't going anywhere. We can explore them any day…." Elsa frowned as she looked around. "Ideally with lots of lanterns and ropes and guards and maybe a couple of experts in castle architecture. The point is …" Elsa picked up Anna's hand. "The point is we have all the time in the world. You know that."

Anna looked at her sister. "I know … it's just … I know you've got so much to do. Running a kingdom is busy work. And I want you to be so happy. And I want to do so many things with you…."

"But I am happy. I really am. It's just …" Elsa mused, " … I'm new to all this. And Mum and Dad … they did everything they could, but it was hard for me to prepare to rule with my powers and having to hide…. So I worry that I'm not as good as they were and I'm trying really hard to catch up … you know?"

"You're doing fine. You really are. But Mum and Dad had each other. You're just one person. But with me helping you … I … Hey …"

Anna trailed off, distracted by something she saw from the corner of her eye. She picked up one of the fallen dresses. "I remember this dress. It … it's …"

Elsa reached out, examining the garment.

The dress was a soft green with a blue pattern dyed into the fabric. "This belonged to Mum. She wore it when we were little. Before I ... before you were hurt."

Anna opened a crate, holding the lantern close so she could see inside. It was filled with books ... familiar books. "All of this ... all of this was Mum's. It must have all been packed away when ..."

Elsa picked up a book and dusted off the cover. "I remember this one. She used to read it to us when we would go to sleep. See? It even has the corner you used to chew on!"

Anna paused, frowning and squinting at the book. "I didn't chew on any book! I ..." She stopped and thought for a minute. "I was young. Books seemed delicious then."

Anna pushed the box away. "I'm sorry, Elsa. I'm your younger sister and I'm supposed to be there for you like Mum and Dad would have been if ... if they hadn't ..." Anna tried to steady her voice. "And once they were gone, I … and …"

Elsa put an arm round her sister comfortingly. "They're not gone. They're right here. They're with us always, in these books and dresses and in our memories – they're all around us. And most importantly, they'll always be with us as long as we have each other."

Anna looked up at her sister. There were tears in her eyes, but she was smiling. "Huh. I guess we found our phantoms, right? I'm always here for you, too, Elsa. I really am."

Elsa reached out and, with a small smile, wiped away the tear that was trickling down Anna's cheek. "And I will always be here for you. And … and I promise: we're going to get out of here and I'm going to take you somewhere and you'll feel so much better about everything. I promise."

Anna felt herself smile. "That … that would mean a lot to me. I think that … Wait…." Anna suddenly stood up, remembering. "You can't take me anywhere tonight, though! *I* have to take *you* somewhere!"

Elsa shook her head. "Well, first things first … we have to get out of here. Agreed?"

Anna looked like she wanted to argue, but instead she nodded. "Agreed. Let's find a way out … and then –"

Anna was opening her mouth to continue when she was interrupted by a nearby screech. Like nails on a chalkboard. Or a cat left on a frozen lake.

It was horrible. Truly horrible.

And it was nearby.

CHAPTER 16

Olaf continued screeching, moaning and howling as loudly as he could while he walked down the rickety staircase. The book on phantoms had said that spirits howled and moaned because they had forgotten how to communicate. Howls were all they understood.

"AAaaeeeeeeEEEAAAHH!" Olaf screeched. *"OOoooohaaaaaAAH!"* he howled.

Down below him, Olaf could see a second stone landing. Below that, the stairs continued down into pitch-black darkness.

Olaf heard a noise. He turned and looked behind him. Hmmm. The staircase sure was wobbling a lot. That was interesting.

CHAPTER 17

Anna ran up the wooden steps with Elsa right behind her. The noise had come from that way; she was sure of it. That meant that whatever had arranged the food in the old dining room and the clothes in the storage room was also that way.

Up and up she ran. The staircase was absurdly high, held up by wooden scaffolding bolted into the walls at intervals. It had clearly been intended as a temporary solution, perhaps for some long-ago maintenance problem, but the work had never been completed. Anna hadn't realized how deep they had gone into the castle basements and how high the castle walls must be, for the two sisters just kept climbing and climbing as the stairs went back and forth and up and up between the walls.

"Anna …" Elsa said between panting breaths as they climbed, "maybe … maybe we should just head back down. There has to be a better way out than this!"

Anna was also exhausted. She gasped as she spoke. "Maybe … maybe there is … but we have to reach the top soon –"

As she said "soon", her foot hit a rotten plank on the stairs and – *crack!* – it gave way beneath her.

"Anna!" Elsa cried out. "Hold on!"

Anna was holding on. She had fallen through a step of the staircase and was wedged into the broken plank at waist level, dangling above a drop that probably stretched all the way back down to the castle basement.

"Why," she managed to say as she struggled not to fall, "do people always tell you to 'hold on' when you're obviously going to hold on? Holding on is the obvious choice!"

Elsa grabbed at Anna's arm, trying to haul her up. "It's meant to be encouraging!"

Anna's feet kicked uselessly in the air. "It's … ergh … very encouraging! Could you also use your powers to maybe –"

Elsa shook her head quickly. "The stairs are already too unstable! The extra weight could cause them to crumble –"

Elsa was cut off by a loud crumbling noise and they both looked down. The staircase was falling apart from the basement up!

Anna felt herself slipping. "Hurry!"

Elsa pulled with all her might and, suddenly, Anna was free, clambering to her feet on the stairs.

"Run!" Anna yelled.

"Now who's pointing out the obvious?" Elsa yelled in return as she ran.

They scrambled, the staircase collapsing behind them. For a moment, Anna felt like she was running on free-floating planks that gravity simply hadn't caught up with. And then, before the sisters could fall, their feet touched stone. It was a small landing jutting out of the castle wall near the very top. It extended for only a few metres and, from there, another rickety staircase descended. Or at least, it had. Both staircases appeared to have crumbled at the same time.

In other words, Anna and Elsa were very precariously perched on a two-metre-long, one-metre-wide stone ledge. A ledge that was icy cold, despite Elsa having avoided using her freezing powers.

And yet the ghost was nowhere to be found.

That was when the laughing began again, echoing off the stone walls that surrounded them.

CHAPTER 18

"Huh," Olaf said as he surveyed the remains of the staircase behind him.

It had happened fast. First the wobbling started; then everything was collapsing. The next thing Olaf knew, he was falling. Luckily, he landed on something soft – that being his bottom – on the second ledge he had seen earlier.

In truth, the experience had tickled. So much so that it had taken him a while to stop laughing after he landed.

Eventually, he got up and made sure all his parts were still attached. It looked like the sheet had helped keep him together. What a great sheet! Adjusting it to make sure his appearance was as ghostly as possible, he looked down. There was still a very long way to the bottom – and no longer any staircase to travel on.

"Huh," he said again. He looked around, considering what to do next.

CHAPTER 19

"Anna …" Elsa said, looking down. "Remember how I said there's no such thing as ghosts?"

Anna nodded. "Yeah. I remember. You said it repeatedly. And yet, here we are. Chasing a phantom through the castle walls."

"Yes. Well –" Elsa nodded – "look down there."

Elsa stepped aside so her sister could see where she was pointing. It was far below them on a ledge very similar to the one Elsa and Anna were on. And the shadows were so deep that they made the … thing … appear almost invisible. But there was no mistaking it. No more pretending it didn't exist – not for Elsa. For at last she had seen what they had been following: a small, sheet-draped spectre of some kind.

"I think," Elsa said, "we just found our –"

BLONG!

"Aah!" cried Elsa, covering her ears.

BLONG!

"So … loud…." stammered Anna, cringing.

BLONG!

"What is that noise?" Elsa heard Anna shout.

BLONG!

"I think …" Elsa began.

BLONG!

"It's …" Elsa continued.

BLONG!

The sisters looked at each other with dawning comprehension.

BLONG!

"The clock!" they shouted, their ears ringing from the tolling of the massive bells.

"We must be near the clock tower!" Anna yelled.

That's when Elsa had a horrible realization. "Seven! It's seven o'clock!"

"Oh, no!" Anna added, seeming to share her sister's horror.

The sisters looked at each other and yelled in unison.

"THE PARTY!"

There was a short pause after that. Elsa looked at Anna. Anna looked at Elsa.

Again in unison, the sisters said, surprised, "Wait! You know?"

Down below, the phantom was waddling along the ledge. *Odd that a ghost might waddle*, Elsa thought.

"Never mind!" she said in a determined tone. "We've been led through these castle walls for too long! It's time we catch that phantom and get where we're supposed to be!"

With that, Elsa waved her hand, and a giant ice slide materialized, starting at their feet and plunging into the shadowy darkness towards the distant ghostly figure.

Anna pointed at the steep and oh-so-very-slippery-looking slide her sister had created.

"You can't be serious."

But she was. Very. And with a grin, Elsa shoved her sister on to the slide. Then, laughing, she jumped down after her.

CHAPTER 20

Olaf was sad. He didn't feel sad very often and it wasn't a feeling he liked very much.

He had been sure there were spirits hiding in the castle walls. Lonely and strange creatures, too shy to step out and find a friend. But instead, he had found only empty rooms and dust.

It was time to accept that he was the only one inside the castle walls.

At that moment, Olaf heard a sound that was a mix between laughter and screams of terror. *Funny*, he thought. *It seems to be getting closer. Maybe ... maybe ...*

This was it.

The spirits were finally showing themselves.

Unnoticed by Olaf, ice slicked over the stone floor at his feet. He turned, arms open, ready to greet his newfound ghostly friends, his sheet billowing as a rush of wind hit him.

And that was when the Princess and the Queen of Arendelle crashed into him and swept him away.

CHAPTER 21

Elsa couldn't believe it. She and her sister had actually captured a phantom! It was amazing!

Less amazing was the fact that they were all still hurtling into the dark.

Now that they had the phantom, Elsa was continuing to conjure the ice-slide down the long narrow corridor, trying to get them to ground level before the spirit could wriggle away.

Unfortunately, the corridor wasn't quite long enough. A dead end loomed out of the darkness just before them.

CHAPTER 22

"Dead end!" Anna called out as she grappled with the spirit. She saw her sister create a huge cushion of snow between them and the fast-approaching wall and she braced for impact.

CHAPTER 23

Elsa, Anna and the ghost all crashed into the snowbank – and discovered that the section of wall behind it wasn't solid at all! The force of the crash popped open a door which was cleverly hidden behind a painting in the Great Hall. The secret door swung wide and through the air they sailed, scattering snow over the heads of dozens of guests, through banners and streamers, until the Queen of Arendelle, her sister – the Princess – and the spirit that had haunted them landed directly in the centre of the largest cake the world had probably ever seen.

After a moment, both cake-covered sisters sat up in the massive dessert, looked around at their surroundings, pointed at each other, then yelled, *"Surprise!"*

They looked at each other in shock.

"Wait … what?" Anna said.

"I'm sorry, I'm confused," Elsa responded.

Then the phantom they had captured popped out of the massive cake between them. "I get it!" the spirit yelled, with a happy laugh not normally associated with such ghostly creatures. "It's a celebration for both of you!"

Anna squinted, feeling confused. Elsa poked at the sheet-covered phantom.

"Is that …" Elsa said.

"I think …" Anna added.

Elsa grabbed the sheet and pulled it off. Anna sighed as the small snowman was revealed underneath. "Yup," she said, relieved. "We've been chasing Olaf."

Shaking her head, Elsa let herself fall backwards into the giant cake with a plop.

A trumpet sounded and confetti floated down from the ceiling. The party had officially started and the celebrations could finally begin.

CHAPTER 24

The amazing dinner-dance was in full swing. What could have been an utter catastrophe had been completely pulled together by the castle staff. As soon as they had realized that the queen and princess were planning surprise events for each other at the same time in the same place, they had taken it upon themselves to combine the events into one ultimate gala. The biggest cake in the world was now even bigger. The streamers were doubled. It was like the most fantastic ball – *plus* the most fantastic banquet.

"Oh. My. Gosh," Anna said, pulling her sister into a relatively quiet corner. "I seriously cannot believe we were both planning surprises

for the same day at the same time! I hope …"
Anna wrung her hands, slightly nervous. "I hope
you like it? I mean … I know … I don't know …"

Elsa hugged her sister. "Are you kidding
me? This is fantastic! It was so sweet of you!
You're always there for me! That's why *I* wanted
to hold an event for *you*. And –" Elsa pulled back
and looked Anna in the eyes – "I wanted to hold
this huge celebration and let you know how much
you mean to me. To the kingdom. You saved me.
You saved … all of us."

Anna blushed a bit as Elsa continued.

"And you're right … what you said in there.
I need you at my side, able to help me with
whatever comes up. I shouldn't try to do
everything by myself. I've just felt like I have so
much to make up for…."

"You don't," Anna said, kindly but firmly.
"You're a good queen. A great queen. You care so
much for everything and everyone … and everyone

knows that! More importantly … Mum and Dad … they would be proud of you."

Elsa smiled. "And they'd be proud of you, too."

The sisters hugged again and afterwards, Anna laughed, flicking away a piece of cake that was still in her hair. "And to think I almost believed we were hunting a real phantom in there! I mean, the dinner table, the dresses and those little footprints we saw … and it was Olaf the entire time!"

Both sisters laughed as Olaf waddled by. The snowman smiled and waved as he headed for the dance floor. "Aw! Look at you guys! So happy! That makes me happy! So we're all happy!"

The sisters laughed. "What about your ghost hunt?" Anna asked. "I'm sorry you didn't find anything, but you ended up leading us to some places with a lot of great memories. So it's not a total loss."

"Oh, that's okay!" Olaf said, waving the concern away. "It would have been nice to find some lonely ghosts and cheer them up and all, but it's even better that I was able to help you guys. Besides," Olaf added as he did a little spin on the floor, "I have a new hobby now. Dancing! And this is just the place to show everyone what an amazing dancer a snowman with snowball feet can be!"

Anna and Elsa laughed as Olaf danced away. Then their laughter slowly trailed off. They stared at each other.

Olaf had big round snowballs for feet. He couldn't have made those footprints.

The mystery of the phantom was still unsolved.

CHAPTER 25

Elsa had tried to be subtle about gathering a small contingent of guards, but word spread like wildfire through the crowd. No one wanted to miss whatever exciting thing was planned next for this very unusual celebration. All the guests were gathered around the mirror where Anna and Elsa had entered the secret passages.

"All right," Queen Elsa commanded in her most royal voice. "Everyone stay back. There is something in these walls, and no one is quite sure what it is. All we know is that it is real. So, everyone, please stay back for your own safety. Olaf, would you please show us how to open the mirror?"

Olaf knocked on the wall next to the mirror.

Nothing happened. "Huh," he said, confused. "That worked before." He tried again, rapping his stick arms against the stone. Still nothing. "It must be stuck," he concluded.

The guards came forward with crowbars to force the hidden door open. As they moved into position, Anna leaned in. "Elsa, are you sure we need to do this? I mean, I know I was the one who was all insistent about the walls being haunted and whatnot, but we were in there for hours and there was nothing –"

Knock. Knock. Knock. A mysterious sound came from behind the mirror.

"I knew it! I knew it!" Olaf shouted happily. "The phantoms are finally answering!"

Elsa nodded to the guard. "Open it. But be careful … and be ready."

With a quick motion, the guards prised the door fully open. The entire gathering watched with breathless anticipation.

Nothing.

"Hmmm," Elsa said, turning to Anna. "I suppose that bit will remain a mystery after all –"

The queen was interrupted by a loud shriek. A squeal, really. A very familiar squeal. A squeal that sounded just like …

"Spy Pig!" Anna yelled as the animal bounded out of the hidden passageway. "*That's* where you've been!"

"But how … how did we not see him? At all!" Elsa responded. "We went everywhere inside those passages!"

Anna hugged the pig. "Because he finally learned to blend with the darkness, just like a mighty shadow boar! Yay, Spy Pig!"

And with that, Elsa, Anna, Olaf and Spy Pig led the way back to the Great Hall, where everyone agreed: it was the greatest ghost- and pig-attended double-surprise dinner dance in history.

THE END

OLAF AND SVEN ON THIN ICE

Written by Elizabeth Rudnick

CHAPTER 1

It was another beautifully perfect day in Arendelle. The blue sky was cloudless and a gentle breeze blew through the warm air, carrying the scent of fresh flowers. It was so perfect, in fact, that it was hard to believe Arendelle had recently been covered in ice and snow.

Back when Princess Elsa of Arendelle was to be crowned queen, something unimaginable had happened. She had accidentally created an icy storm and covered the kingdom in snow! What no one – not even her sister, Princess Anna – had known at the time was that Elsa had special powers. Unfortunately, she couldn't always control those powers. Horrified by what she had done to Arendelle, Elsa ran away and created an ice palace far up on the North Mountain. She vowed she would never return to Arendelle, so that everyone, especially her sister, would be safe from her icy magic.

The only problem was that after Elsa left Arendelle, it continued to snow … and snow … and snow some more. It snowed until the entire town was covered in white and every person and animal was cold through and through. To stop the snow, someone had to find Elsa.

Luckily, Princess Anna was brave and clever. With the help of some new friends, like Kristoff – who sold ice for a living – his friend, Sven the reindeer, and a snowman named Olaf, she saved the day. Anna found her sister and showed her that love was stronger than fear. Elsa returned to Arendelle and thawed the kingdom. In no time at all, the people of Arendelle learned to love and appreciate their new queen.

Queen Elsa, Anna and the townspeople of Arendelle were ready to embark on this new era in the kingdom. The royal sisters now kept the castle gates open and the sound of laughter always echoed through the halls.

But on this particular morning, singing, not laughing, could be heard in the palace. The tune was slightly off-key but cheery and contagious. The singer was Olaf – the friendly snowman Elsa had created when she built her ice palace. He looked just like a snowman the sisters had made when they were children – only now he was alive and could talk!

Olaf had been living in the castle for just a short while, but everyone loved the happy-go-lucky snowman.

As Olaf made his way through the halls, he zigzagged a bit. The little snowman wasn't particularly good at moving in a straight line. "This way, I get to see things that other people miss when they only walk straight," the always-optimistic Olaf had said when Princess Anna once pointed out his slight wobble. "You should try it, Anna. I bet you'd like it."

At the moment, he was looking for his friend Princess Anna. They were supposed to go into town and find a special present for the royal cook. The next day was her birthday and Olaf loved picking out presents. Maybe they would get her a new apron. Or a nice new spatula! Pausing to think, Olaf raised one of his stick hands to his long carrot nose. That gave him an idea. Maybe Cook would like a basket of freshly picked vegetables? Then Olaf shook his head. Cook had plenty of vegetables. She needed something special. She needed a treat on her birthday! "Maybe we can get her an ice-cream cake," Olaf thought aloud. "Yes, an ice-cream cake sounds delicious. Nice and cold and full of yummy goodness. Ice-cream cake on a warm day … it'll melt just a little and then be perfect. Cook will definitely love it!"

Hearing voices ahead, Olaf quickened his pace and found himself on one of the castle's many balconies. Zigzagging closer to the large stone railing, he poked his nose through and peered down into the room below. His eyes lit up. It was Princess Anna and Kristoff! "Oh! My favourite friends!" he squealed. Just as he was about to shout hello, he stopped. Anna had crossed her arms and was frowning.

"I know it isn't what we talked about," Olaf heard Kristoff say, "but it's going to be great. You, me, a picnic basket full of food! Just think … we get to spend the whole day together!"

Olaf saw Anna's expression soften slightly and a smile spread across her face. He sighed. *Phew!* He liked it much better when everyone was smiling. Then Olaf let out a tiny gasp. *Wait!* he thought. *Kristoff and Anna are going on a picnic?*

Today? But Kristoff was supposed to deliver ice today! It was his job as the Official Arendelle Ice Master and Deliverer. If Kristoff didn't make his deliveries, the townspeople wouldn't have ice – and it was going to be a beautiful but awfully warm day. Olaf's eyes grew wide. This was worse than he had first thought. Olaf couldn't possibly keep the cook's ice-cream cake cold without ice.

Olaf walked back and forth and up and down the hallway. He had to think of something. If Kristoff couldn't deliver ice, who could?

And then Olaf had a fantastic idea. He would go and get the ice and deliver it himself! Yes! It would be perfect. Kristoff and Anna would enjoy their picnic, Cook would get her birthday cake, the people of Arendelle would get their ice, and *Olaf* would get to be the Official Substitute Arendelle Ice Master and Deliverer for the day!

CHAPTER 2

Now that Olaf had the idea, he was ready to go! He knew that Kristoff got ice blocks from a special lake on a mountain that overlooked Arendelle. He also knew that Kristoff usually started his day very early. Olaf looked at the sun, which was quickly rising in the sky. He needed to get going! There was just one teensy, tiny problem. He was a not a very large snowman. How was he going to deliver the ice all by himself?

Then Olaf had his second fantastic idea of the day. He would get his good friend Sven the reindeer to help! Sven would know where the special lake was, how to get the ice blocks and which townspeople needed ice. Best of all, he was a reindeer and it was a known fact that reindeer were usually stronger than snowmen. Then Olaf remembered his friend Marshmallow. *Maybe he can help, too!* Olaf thought.

Letting out an excited yelp, Olaf turned and headed towards the royal stables. Unfortunately, a snowman can only move so fast. Olaf wibbled and wobbled and zigged and zagged, but still, it was rather slow-going. And then there was the small issue of Olaf's attention span. It was very, very short.

Bumping down the stairs, he got distracted by a pretty new painting of Queen Elsa. "She is just so beautiful," Olaf said, clapping his hands together. "I wonder what she's doing today. Maybe she'd want to pick flowers with me. No, no, no. What am I thinking? Think ice, Olaf. Ice, ice, ice," he muttered to himself.

Finally, Olaf made it to the stables, where he found Sven in his stall, happily munching on hay.

Raising his head, Sven saw Olaf. "Harrumph?" Sven the reindeer grunted in greeting.

"Sven! My pal!" Olaf cried. "It's been forever. You sure are looking handsome today. Did you shine your antlers?"

Sven raised a hairy eyebrow. What was Olaf talking about? He had just seen him the day before. "Heerum?" Sven snorted. That was reindeer for "Why are you here?"

"I was just getting to that," Olaf answered. "I have the best news ever. *I* am going to be the Official Substitute Arendelle Ice Master and Deliverer for the day. And *you* are going to help me," he said proudly. Then he filled Sven in. He told him all about Kristoff's day off and the brilliant plan he had come up with. "I can't do it alone, Sven. I need you to show me the ropes. We'll be the best substitute ice team there ever was!"

Sven wasn't so sure. He knew Kristoff was very particular about his ice deliveries. Still, Olaf said this would help Kristoff – and Sven always wanted to help Kristoff. He loved him more than anything in the world ... more than fresh grass and even more than carrots! Speaking of which.... He eyed Olaf's nose and the snowman smiled, clueless that Sven was hoping for a quick snack. Looking at the hopeful expression in Olaf's eyes, the reindeer let out a sigh. Then he nodded, his antlers nearly knocking over Olaf.

"So you'll do it?" Olaf cried happily. "I knew you would help me! This is going to be a great day! Let's get going." He turned to head out of the stables and once again began to sing: "We're going on an adventure, we're going on an adventure. A great, big, grand adventure!" He had almost reached the stable door when he realized he didn't hear the *clip-clop* of reindeer hooves behind him. Olaf stopped and turned round.

Sven was still standing in his stall. Dangling from his mouth was a large leather harness.

The harness was supposed to attach Sven's halter to the sleigh. Sven swung his head back and forth as if to say, "You're forgetting something!" *That's how Kristoff carries so much ice down from the mountain*, Olaf thought.

"Silly me!" said Olaf. "We can't carry ice without a sleigh! Thanks, Sven. See? We are already working like a team."

He walked back to Sven and stood in front of him. The reindeer dropped the harness on the ground in front of Olaf. Then he lowered his head and waited for Olaf to put it on.

Olaf looked down at the harness. Then he raised his short stick arms. They barely reached Sven's knees. Then he looked up at the reindeer's back. He looked way, way, *way* up. "Have you grown?" Olaf asked. "I don't remember you being this tall."

The reindeer shook his head.

"Don't worry, pal! It doesn't matter, because tall is good! Really good, in fact," Olaf said.

He began walking from one side of Sven to the other, considering how to place the harness on Sven's back. "Maybe … or maybe … hmmm…. So many possibilities, Sven! I just need to figure out which one is best!"

Sven watched for a while and then shook his head. He already had a plan that would work! Lowering his head, Sven once again grabbed the harness in his teeth. Then he swung his head up and down. The harness began to sway back and forth. Sven kept nodding and the harness swung faster and higher. With one last nod, it swung back and then up, up, up until it flipped over Sven's head and landed on his back. He let out a loud "HARRUMPH!"

Olaf looked up. "Yippee!" he cheered, clapping his stick arms together. "You are the smartest, most brilliant-est reindeer there ever was." Then Olaf hooked the straps hanging below Sven's belly together. "Is that it? Are we ready to go now?" he asked.

Sven shook his head. There was one more step. He nodded his antlers towards the wooden sleigh to remind Olaf. Luckily, hooking the harness to the sleigh was fairly straightforward and soon the job was complete.

Kneeling down, Sven let Olaf climb on to his back. They would be able to get the ice and make all the deliveries much more quickly with Olaf riding Sven. After all, reindeers were usually faster than snowmen.

"Off we go!" Olaf cried.

With a grunt, Sven made his way out of the stable and, together, they headed towards Arendelle's main gate. Their ice-adventure had officially begun!

CHAPTER 3

"This is going to be the absolute best day ever!" Olaf said as Sven walked along. "Wait. Going to the beach would be the best day ever. But if I went to the beach, I wouldn't be able to help Kristoff and Anna, my best friends in the whole wide world."

Sven stopped in his tracks, nearly tossing the snowman to the ground. Then he looked over his shoulder and narrowed his eyes. "Hmmmump?"

"Oh, Sven! I'm sorry! Of *course* you are one of my best friends, too."

Sven let out a pleased snort and resumed walking. Olaf resumed talking.

"Anyhoo, I just love today. First we'll head up to the mountain. Then we'll start …"

Olaf's voice faded as he saw one of the boys who worked in the stables coming towards them. The boy was kicking rocks as he walked, so he didn't realize Olaf and Sven were there until he was practically right on top of them.

"Oh!" he gasped.

"Hi!" Olaf cried.

"Harrumph!" Sven harrumphed.

"I didn't see you," the stable boy apologized. Then he noticed that there was a snowman on top of a reindeer. And a cloud on top of a snowman. And the reindeer was dragging a sleigh used for collecting ice blocks. It was an unusual sight. "Um, what are you doing?" the boy finally asked.

Olaf puffed up his chest. He tried to make his expression as serious as possible. "*I* am the Official Substitute Arendelle Ice Master and Deliverer and I happen to be saving the day."

"Harrumph?" Sven grunted, turning to give Olaf a look.

"I'm sorry, Sven. I meant *we* happen to be saving the day," Olaf said. Then he turned back to the boy. "We are going to pick up ice blocks from the lake and make all of Kristoff's deliveries for him."

The stable boy looked at Olaf's stick arms. "How are you going to do that? You're just a snowman."

Olaf's eyes widened. "*Just* a snowman?" he repeated. "What do you think snowmen are made of?" The boy shrugged. "Snow, of course! Snowmen know all about ice and snow."

The stable boy had to give Olaf credit: he was determined. *Maybe it will work out*, he thought. *It's a big maybe, though.* So with a "good luck" and a wave, the young boy sent them on their way.

"See, Sven?" Olaf said happily. "People love me!"

The reindeer let out a snort.

As they continued towards Arendelle's main gate, they passed various shops. Several of the shopkeepers came out to see what was going on. They were surprised to see Sven without Kristoff.

"What are you doing here, Olaf?" the baker asked. "Where's Kristoff? Isn't he supposed to be delivering ice today?"

"Not today! Today *I* will be your Official Substitute Arendelle Ice Master and Deliverer!" Olaf announced proudly.

"Official Substitute Ice Master?" the baker repeated. "What does that mean? How can a little snowman get all the ice the townspeople need?"

Olaf smiled. "I may be little, but I have a big heart," he replied. "And Sven is a very big reindeer. Together, the two of us will be as strong as one Kristoff. Maybe even stronger! Do not fear, Mr Baker Man! You will have your ice ... I promise!"

With a wave of Olaf's stick arm, Olaf and Sven continued along. It didn't take long for news of Olaf delivering the ice to spread through the town. Soon everyone was asking questions like "What are you doing, Olaf?" or "Why are you riding Sven?" or "Where's Kristoff today?"

And every time, Olaf would smile and say, "Don't fret, dear Arendellians! I am your Official Substitute Arendelle Ice Master and Deliverer! Your ice is in good hands!" No matter how many people asked and no matter how many times people expressed their doubts about him, Olaf stayed positive. He wouldn't let Arendelle down. He took his job very seriously. After all, he was the *Official* Substitute Arendelle Ice Master and Deliverer – and that meant something.

As they finally began their trek up to the mountain, Olaf turned and shouted back into town, "I'll see you soon! The Official Substitute Arendelle Ice Master and Deliverer and the best reindeer around are on the job!"

CHAPTER 4

As Olaf and Sven made their way out of Arendelle, the townspeople were all atwitter. Except for the time Queen Elsa's magical secret was revealed, day-to-day life in Arendelle was mostly routine and didn't hold too many surprises. The baker baked. The dressmaker sewed. The woodchopper chopped. And Kristoff – not Olaf – delivered the ice.

"I hope the snowman doesn't get lost," an elderly woman said. "He's such a cute little guy."

"Or what if something happens to the sleigh?" a man asked. "We could go *days* without ice!"

As the town continued to discuss this new development, Kristoff made his way to the stables.

He was unaware that Olaf had overheard him talking to Anna and that Olaf had wrongly presumed Kristoff was taking the day off. So he was rather surprised when he walked into the stables and Sven was nowhere to be found.

"Sven?" he called out. No 'harrumph' came in response. Kristoff frowned. "We don't have time to play hide-and-seek today, buddy. We're running late as it is."

Still no noise from Sven.

Growing worried, Kristoff peered into every stall. Then he looked in the pasture. He even looked in the tack room. No Sven! Then he caught sight of a stable boy.

"Hey!" Kristoff shouted, startling the boy. "Do you know where Sven is?"

The boy looked at him blankly. He was new to the stable, so he didn't know everyone yet.

"My reindeer?" Kristoff added.

The boy's eyes lit up. "The reindeer with the

snowman! Yeah, I know where they are. Well, I know where they *were*."

"And that would be …"

"They were going for ice. The snowman said he was the Official Substitute Arendelle Ice Master and Deliverer. Although I don't know how he'll deliver ice with those little arms and …"

Kristoff didn't wait to hear what else the stable boy had to say. He turned and ran towards town. As he sped along, he muttered to himself: "Why would Olaf decide to deliver ice? And why would Sven go along with it? What if they get hurt? Or lost?" He ran quickly, hoping he could catch up with them soon!

Reaching the centre of town, he was bombarded by people telling him about Olaf's adventure. He pushed his way through the crowd and raced to the gate. On the ground he could just make out familiar hoofprints. Kristoff saw that Olaf and Sven were headed towards the North Mountain.

It looked like he was going to have to play catch-up. He could only hope that he would find Olaf and Sven before they turned a tiny inconvenience into a big slushy one.

CHAPTER 5

Olaf was having so much fun on his adventure with Sven! In fact, the duo was making good time as Sven marched up the mountain. With the sleigh empty and only a little snowman to carry, the work was easy for the reindeer. So Sven used the time to take in his surroundings.

Up on Sven's back, Olaf was enjoying the scenery, too. He hadn't been on the mountain for some time. It was nice to see that the trees were full of leaves and the grass underneath Sven's hooves was bright green. Birds chirped and every so often a squirrel or rabbit would peek its head out and watch them as they passed by.

Finally, after they had walked for quite a while, the forest began to thin. The air got colder and soon they found that the ground was no longer green, but white with snow. "Look at that, Sven! We must be almost there," Olaf said. The reindeer let out a pleased harrumph. "Now we just need to find the lake," Olaf said cheerily.

With a nod, Sven pulled the sleigh along, turning this way and that. He knew the route well and, after a few minutes, they arrived at the lake.

Letting out a happy yelp, Olaf jumped off Sven's back, unhooked his friend from the sleigh and quickly made his way to the edge of the lake. Sven followed close behind.

Both Olaf and Sven were surprised by what they found: they didn't have to worry about cutting any ice blocks, because a huge pile had already been cut and the blocks were scattered along the shore! "We're so lucky, Sven!" Olaf said. "Kristoff must have cut too many blocks on his last trip – which means we can just deliver them today. This will be so easy!"

Of course, there was another teensy, tiny problem that wasn't very teensy and wasn't very tiny. Kristoff's blocks of ice were very big and very heavy. How would Olaf and Sven be able to gather them all up and put them in the sleigh?

Sven watched as Olaf walked around and mumbled to himself about all the possibilities. Sven knew his snowman friend could come up with some inventive ideas, but he also knew that Olaf didn't have to figure out this one alone. It was just like when Kristoff was younger and needed Sven's help to gather ice. Sometimes it went smoothly; sometimes one of them ended up wet and cold. However, working as a team always, well, worked. Sven and Olaf could work together, too.

Sven walked over to Olaf and let out a loud "Harrumph."

The snowman stopped. "What is it, Sven? Can't you see I'm trying to figure out how the Official Substitute Arendelle Ice Master and Deliverer should collect the ice?"

"Harrumph!" Sven replied.

"Oh, you have an idea?" Olaf asked.

Sven nodded. He shook his big body, causing the harness buckles to jangle. Then he pointed his antlers at the ice.

Olaf laughed. "I don't think we should stop and play a game right now! But maybe later, okay?"

Once again, Sven shook his harness. And again he pointed his antlers at the ice. Olaf still wasn't getting it, so Sven pawed at the snow, drawing a semicircle with his front hoof. Finally, he looked back at his harness.

"Oh, I see!" Olaf squealed. "You think we should take the harness and turn it into a loop?"

Sven nodded.

"And then we will use the loop to pull the ice?"

Again Sven nodded.

"Sven, you're a genius! I knew we would make a great team!"

The reindeer puffed up his chest proudly.

"Let's get to work!" Olaf exclaimed.

Sven knelt down next to Olaf, who reached out for the harness buckles. Sven waited patiently as the snowman fastened the straps. "Look at us, Sven! Kristoff is going to be so proud. I hope he and Anna are having a nice time on their picnic."

When Olaf was done fastening the straps and talking about how fun today was turning out to be, Sven was happy to see the harness was connected so that it created a perfect loop. He picked up the loop in his teeth and dragged it over to a medium-sized block of ice.

As he had done in the stables, Sven nodded his head up and down until finally, with one big last nod, he looped a block of ice. He pulled it to the sleigh. Then he did it again, and again, and again until they had a large pile of ice blocks ready to be loaded on to the sleigh.

"Thanks, Sven!" Olaf said when the reindeer was done. "I can take it from here." He scurried over to the first block. He brushed his hands off. He placed them on the ice. And he pushed and he shoved. Then he pushed and shoved some more. The ice didn't budge. "Don't worry, Sven. I think this piece is just stuck in a rut. I'll try another."

Olaf walked over to a second block of ice. Then he pushed. He shoved. And he pushed and shoved some more. Just like before, the ice didn't budge. He pushed each block and each time there was the same result. Olaf was just not strong enough to move the ice.

Luckily, while Olaf was busy trying to push the ice, Sven had also been busy. Knowing that Olaf probably couldn't lift the ice blocks, Sven was trying something different. He found two fallen logs and, using his antlers, pushed them together so they were propped at an angle against the sleigh, creating a ramp. Then he walked back to Olaf, who was still vainly pushing a block of ice.

"Harrumph?" he snorted.

"You want to help? Sure, that'd be great!" Olaf said.

So Sven showed him. Leaning his large head down, he began to push one of the blocks with his antlers. Slowly at first and then faster, the ice began to move forward, until Sven had pushed it close to the ramp. Then, placing the tips of his antlers underneath the ice, he lifted the block up on to the log ramp. After that he simply had to push it up the ramp until it landed in the wagon.

"Sven!" Olaf cried. "What a smart reindeer you are! We are the best official substitute ice team there ever was!"

Together – or rather with Sven pushing and Olaf trying his best – they loaded another block into the sleigh. Then another. "Look at us go!" Olaf shouted as they worked. "We're the best!

Up we go. Push that ice! Push, push, PUSH!" When the final block of ice was loaded, Olaf let out a big breath. "*Whew!* What a workout! I'm exhausted."

His chest heaving, Sven looked at the snowman. "Hmmmph!" which roughly translated to "Are you kidding me?"

Olaf smiled. "Of course I meant *you* were getting the workout, Sven. But all that cheering was exhausting, too."

The reindeer thought about it for a moment and then nodded. His little snowy friend *had* helped him stay motivated.

Hopping on to Sven's back, Olaf gave the signal. Together, they headed out, Olaf singing and Sven bobbing his head in time with Olaf's slightly off-key tune. They were ready to make their first delivery!

CHAPTER 6

Luckily, their first stop was not far away. In no time, they reached Wandering Oaken's Trading Post and Sauna. The trading post happened to be the only place in the area with a sauna, which made it a popular destination all year round, so Oaken depended on Kristoff's ice delivery to keep the drinks and food cold for his guests.

As Olaf and Sven pulled up in front of the trading post, Oaken stepped out on to the front porch. He was a very large man with a bushy beard, bright red hair and rosy cheeks. He squinted at the pair in confusion. "Hoo-hoo!" he called out. "Kristoff? You look quite different!" he joked with the snowman.

"I'm not Kristoff!" Olaf said cheerfully. "I'm the Official Substitute Arendelle Ice Master and Deliverer and this is my Official Substitute Arendelle Ice Reindeer." He paused. "Actually, Sven is always the ice reindeer, but you know what I mean. We are the substitute ice team, here to help with all your ice needs!" Olaf went on cheerfully. "Where should we put your ice?"

Oaken had seen plenty of strange things at the trading post, so a snowman riding a reindeer and delivering ice didn't faze him. Oaken pointed to a pair of smaller buildings behind the trading post. "Please unload the ice in the shed," he said. "When you are done, I will bring your payment."

"Let's go, Sven!" Olaf said. "Time to deliver the ice!" Sven began to walk round to the back.

As they approached the first building, Sven slowed down. "What are you doing, Sven?" Olaf asked. "We're supposed to put the ice in the *shed*. Clearly, that is an *outbuilding*. Keep going!"

Sven didn't move.

"Hee-ya!" Olaf shouted, trying to get the reindeer to continue walking.

Still, Sven didn't move.

"Do you want to play a fun game?" Olaf asked. "Or is it a treat you're after? Soon, I promise! We just need to deliver this ice to the shed, okay?"

The reindeer let out a big sigh. "Harrumph," he snorted, as if to say, "This is not a good idea." He knew that Kristoff usually dropped off the ice at the first building – but Olaf kept insisting that Oaken wanted it in the second building. Finally, Sven walked to the other building and halted in front of the door.

"Fantastic!" Olaf exclaimed. "Now if you help with the ramp, I'll push the ice out of the sleigh. Look how good we are at this, Sven!"

Again, Sven pushed the logs into place so they lined up with the blocks of ice. The stacks of ice had created a slick surface that made it easy for Olaf to slide the top blocks off the wagon.

Quickly, Olaf gave a heave – and a few big cold blocks tumbled down the ramp, pushed open the doors of the building and rumbled inside.

"And there you have it!" Olaf said, clapping his hands together. "See how easy that was, Sven? I *love* being the Official Substitute Arendelle Ice Master and Deliverer!"

Sven harrumphed sceptically, but Olaf didn't hear. "Do you think Kristoff would let me help more often?" he mused.

Sven stared at the closed door of the trading post with a worried expression on his fuzzy face. But Olaf was thrilled. They had completed the first ice delivery of the day!

CHAPTER 7

Kristoff was a bit tired. He had hiked all the way up to the lake only to find that he had just missed Olaf and Sven. From the look of things, they had succeeded in collecting some of the ice he'd left after his last trip. Kristoff had to admit he hadn't expected Olaf to make it that far, let alone figure out a way to load the ice. *Pretty impressive,* Kristoff thought. But he didn't hang around the lake admiring their work for too long. He wanted to catch up with Olaf and Sven before they arrived at their next destination. It wasn't difficult to find their tracks and soon he was following their route back down the mountain.

Arriving at Wandering Oaken's Trading Post and Sauna, Kristoff glanced around, looking for the snowman and the reindeer. He didn't see them. What he *did* see was Oaken standing in front of a building, out of which steam was billowing.

When Oaken saw Kristoff, his face turned slightly redder than normal. "Hoo-hoo! Kristoff!" the big man called. "I missed you very much today! That snowman is *not* the ice master and deliverer that you are."

Kristoff took a step back. *Uh-oh,* he thought. *What happened?*

As Oaken walked past him towards the steaming shed, Kristoff could see the man was upset. When he opened the doors, Kristoff could see why.

The building was the trading post's sauna. Or what *had* been the sauna. Now it was just a wet mess. The reason was clear: sitting there, in the centre of the room, was the last bit of a melting block of ice. When Olaf had pushed the ice into the building, it had landed right in the middle of the fire that kept the sauna stones hot. Immediately, they had begun to cool and the ice had begun to melt! The sauna was now cold instead of hot and steamy.

Kristoff gulped. "I'm sorry, Oaken!" he said. "I didn't know Olaf was trying to deliver the ice by himself. What can I do to make things right?"

"You can help me mop up the sauna and rebuild that fire," Oaken replied. "And then maybe you can deliver me twice the usual amount of ice next time. What do you say?"

There was nothing Kristoff could do but agree. As he went to find a mop, he let out a long, deep groan. The day was not going according to plan. And he knew Olaf and Sven would be making more deliveries, which meant Kristoff had to hurry to catch up to them before anything else happened!

CHAPTER 8

As Kristoff got to work cleaning up Olaf's mess, the snowman was happily making his way towards the next stop on the ice-delivery route – Troll Valley.

"I love visiting the trolls, don't you, Sven?" Olaf said cheerfully.

The reindeer raised an eyebrow. Then he snorted loudly.

"Oh, right! We talked about treats! Maybe the trolls will have something for you to nibble on." But as he spoke, his eyes grew wide. He had just had another brilliant idea. "You know what? Troll Valley *is* kind of far away. Maybe we should stop now so you can have a little snack. What do you think?"

The reindeer shook his head. Then he nodded his antlers to the right. Following his gaze, Olaf saw the North Mountain. It towered high above them, the top covered in snow year-round.

The North Mountain was where Elsa had made her ice palace when she ran away from Arendelle. It had been beautiful. It had also been isolated. No one had lived there except for Elsa – and Marshmallow. The huge creature was made of snow and ice. He was very strong and last time Olaf and Sven had run into him, he had not been happy. He had even tried to throw Olaf over a cliff! Olaf still thought Marshmallow had just been having a bad day. He only had nice things to say about Marshmallow!

But that didn't mean Sven was ready to run into Marshmallow again. Unfortunately, there was no way to get to Troll Valley without passing the large mountain. Every time he and Kristoff had gone that way, they had hurried through as fast as possible.

"Oh, Sven! Don't worry!" Olaf said, not the least bit concerned about Marshmallow. "Look! There's a perfect lake to sit by and have a quick nibble. How could you and Kristoff have missed this place?"

"Harrumph!" Sven snorted. They hadn't *missed* it, was what his snort meant. They had just chosen not to use it because it was too close to Marshmallow's territory.

Olaf smiled at Sven. He knew exactly what the reindeer's snort had meant. "That's just silly," he said. "It is a perfectly perfect lake and Marshmallow is not such a bad guy. I bet he would be so happy to see us now! He is probably pretty lonely, you know. I mean, the big guy is up here all alone now that Elsa is in Arendelle. He has no one to play games with or talk to or sit and read with." Olaf put a hand to his chest in sympathy. "Sven, I feel bad for Marshmallow. I think we should go and find him and invite him to join us."

Sven shook his head.

"Fine," Olaf said. "I'll just come back by myself sometime." Then he added, "I bet someday you, Marshmallow and I will get together, though. We could have an amazing snowball fight – or better yet … we can all go to the beach together!"

Sven shook his head and then began to pull the sleigh a little further away from the lake.

"No, no!" Olaf cried. "Come on, pal! We will just take a quick break and you can have your much-needed snack."

Together Olaf and Sven made their way to the lake. The snowman whistled as they went, not a care in the world. But Sven walked very slowly and very softly. When Olaf made a particularly high-pitched whistle, Sven cringed. And when he heard a twig snap in the nearby woods, he nearly jumped out of his skin. He was sure that at any minute, a very angry Marshmallow would appear. He even thought he saw Marshmallow in the distance looking down from the ice palace. He wasn't positive, but he certainly quickened his pace.

After what felt like an eternity to Sven, the pair arrived at the shore of the lovely lake. Olaf hopped off Sven's back. Then he clapped his little stick hands together. "Time to relax!"

CHAPTER 9

The sun was beginning its descent towards the horizon. They had to get their final deliveries made before it was dark. Still, Olaf wanted to make sure Sven ate. He didn't want his friend getting too hungry. Being the reindeer helper for the Official Substitute Arendelle Ice Master and Deliverer was hard work.

He wobbled to the back of the sleigh and pulled out a little sack filled with treats from the cook. He had made sure to stop in the kitchen before leaving the palace. Olaf always liked to be prepared.

"Look, Sven! I made sure Cook gave you some carrots and a loaf of bread. And she packed another extra treat – a carrot snowflake! Isn't she clever?" The reindeer's big ears perked up. "She made a snowflake out of carrots. She definitely deserves a great birthday gift."

Sven's belly let out a loud rumble. Maybe a snack stop wasn't such a bad idea after all.

Olaf rummaged around in his sack. Pulling out the hunk of bread, he smiled. "Now, I'm just going to start a little fire. Kristoff says Cook's bread always tastes better toasted."

"Harrumph?" Sven replied.

"Of course I know how to build a fire," Olaf answered. "You'll see. I love a nice fire. It is almost as great as lying on a sandy beach. All warm and toasty."

As Sven watched, the tiny snowman collected some twigs and leaves and built a small fire. He couldn't find a match, so he rubbed two little sticks together until he started to see smoke. When the flames were flickering merrily, Olaf sat down. Then he inched closer to the fire.

Then closer still. Soon he was right next to the hot flames.

Sven snorted a warning.

"What's wrong?" Olaf asked. "Marshmallow is nowhere to be found. We are perfectly safe and I'm perfectly toasty by the fire. I just have to remember not to get too ... whoa, too close, too close!" Olaf yelled as he looked down and realized his nose was where his mouth used to be and his mouth was where his buttons had been. He was melting!

Hopping up, Olaf tried to hold his face together before he completely melted. He started dancing around, trying to save his buttons! Fortunately, his flurry was there to keep him cold. Unfortunately, as he danced about, he got too close to the flames and one of his stick arms caught fire!

"This is really hot!" Olaf shouted.

"HARRUMPHHHH!" Sven snorted. "Hara! Um! PHHH!" Quickly, Sven stepped forward and pushed the little snowman down with his nose so that Olaf was rolling in the snow. The flames were extinguished, but Olaf continued to roll. Then he began to roll faster. And faster. And faster still!

As Sven watched, the tiny snowman grew into a large snowman. Then he grew into a really, really large snowman!

With a loud *THUNK*, Olaf reached the bottom of the hill and hit a small fir tree. His new layers of snow fell off and he sat there, once again small and now a little bit dazed. Looking down, he saw that his arm was singed, but luckily, the snow had put out the fire before it could do any real damage.

"Well, that was unexpected," Olaf said. Then he laughed. "Let's do it again!"

Sighing, Sven kicked some snow on to the fire and walked down towards Olaf. It seemed like a good time to move on to Troll Valley.

CHAPTER 10

"I knew what I was doing, you know," Olaf explained as they walked along. "It was fun, Sven! I do love heat! Plus, I got a nice new snow bath. Snowmen like to add layers every once in a while to freshen up. It makes our original layers cleaner." He puffed out his chest. "Don't I look cleaner?"

Sven snorted sceptically.

"Well, I feel fantastic," Olaf said. "A roll in the snow might help you, too."

In response, Sven stopped short and shook himself violently. Olaf had to hold on tight not to get thrown off.

His point made, Sven continued to drag the sleigh towards Troll Valley. Soon they arrived at the entrance. The landscape was dotted with what looked like rocks of varying sizes and shapes, covered with green moss. The trees were tall, their branches covered in thick leaves. The valley was low enough on the mountain range not to be covered in snow year-round, but the air was still crisp.

Coming to a stop, Sven let out a loud snort.

For a moment, nothing happened. Then, one by one, the rocks began to rumble. Then they began to shake. Suddenly, the rocks began to roll until, finally, they transformed into trolls!

The trolls all let out happy shouts when they saw the duo and within moments Olaf and Sven were surrounded. "Sven! Olaf! We've missed you!" one troll shouted.

"Hi there!" Olaf called, turning to the clamouring troll babies. "Why, ha-ha! That tickles!"

As Olaf played with some of the troll babies, a few of the other trolls ran up and hugged Sven's legs. Several began to plait the longer hair on his neck.

A couple of trolls even climbed into the sleigh and sat on the ice. A snort from Sven stopped them short, though, and sheepishly they climbed down.

Finally, after nearly every troll had said hello, Bulda and Cliff made their way over to Sven. They had practically raised Kristoff and were extremely fond of him and his reindeer.

"Where's Kristoff?" Bulda asked.

"Harrumph," Sven snorted, nodding over his shoulder at Olaf. He snorted a few more times before Bulda's eyes lit up.

She clapped her hands together happily. "Olaf, how sweet of you to help Kristoff out! He and his pretty Anna should always spend time together when they can. Are they both doing well?"

Before Olaf could reply, Cliff let out a big rumbly laugh. "Of course they are, Bulda!" he said. "Such a great pair! I always told Kristoff he would find himself a nice girl and settle down. No need to spend all your time with a reindeer."

Sven snorted, spraying Cliff.

The troll let out a laugh. "Not that you aren't great company, Sven."

Sven nodded and then nuzzled his head against the little troll.

"Well, since you are here," Bulda said, "Sven, would you like a snack? And, Olaf, I'm sure the troll babies would love one of your stories!"

"Oh, you bet!" Olaf cheered. "I have the perfect story about my favourite thing in the whole wide world … summer, of course!" As he started to walk away, Sven stopped him with a "Harrumph".

Olaf turned to his reindeer friend and said, "Sven, you lucky reindeer! Two snacks in one day! I love coming to visit friends!"

But that wasn't what Sven's "harrumph" had meant. Sven looked back at the sleigh and the blocks of ice sitting inside. Then he looked up at the sun. He looked back down at Olaf and shook his head.

They were no longer up in the North Mountain, so the ice might melt if they stayed for too long.

"You worry too much, Sven. Just wait here and enjoy your snack. I'll be back soon!"

As the snowman turned to go, Sven looked up at the sun one more time. *What could go wrong in a few minutes?* he thought.

CHAPTER 11

A lot, it seemed, could go wrong in a few minutes – if a few minutes turned into an hour. And if in that hour a sleigh full of ice sat out in the sun.

Arriving back at the sleigh, Sven noticed that they barely had any ice blocks left and the ice blocks they did have were getting smaller by the minute.

"Is there a problem?" Olaf said when he saw Sven giving him a look. "These small pieces are so cute – they'll work out great!"

Climbing on to Sven's back, Olaf waved goodbye to the trolls and promised to return soon. Then he and Sven headed out of Troll Valley towards their second-to-last stop.

Behind them, the trolls waved and waved.

Finally, one by one they lowered their hands as Olaf and Sven disappeared into the forest. But soon one of the trolls realized that her young son was nowhere to be found! She began to call out his name: "Pebble? Pebble!"

The trolls began the search for Pebble as Olaf and Sven made their way closer and closer to Arendelle.

"We're almost done!" Olaf said excitedly. "We have just enough ice, too." He turned round to double-check and Olaf saw two little eyes peering over an ice block.

"Ahh!" Olaf cried, delighted that Pebble had joined them.

"Ahh!" Pebble shouted, mimicking the happy-go-lucky snowman.

"Harrumph?" Sven snorted, coming to a stop.

"Hi there, Pebble!" Olaf said. "I don't think you're supposed to be joining us, but I sure am glad to see you!"

Pebble's eyes watered. "I just wanted to go for a little ride. Don't be mad, please?"

Olaf couldn't stand to see anyone cry, especially an adorable little troll. Glancing over his shoulder, he said, "Well, Sven, looks like we have a new member on our team." Looking back at Pebble, he added, "We can take you home after we finish the deliveries. So until then, just hang tight."

"Thanks, Olaf!" Pebble cried, leaping up and plopping himself down behind Olaf. Then he began to sing a happy little tune. Soon Olaf was singing, too. It was nice to have another friend along.

"I am also a fabulous babysitter," Olaf told Sven. "Pebble's parents have nothing to worry about. Nothing at all."

CHAPTER 12

Unfortunately, Kristoff had just missed Olaf and Sven at Troll Valley. Instead, he was met by a group of frantic trolls.

Kristoff had already been expecting the worst. Following Sven's tracks, he had come upon the remains of a fire and what looked liked the aftermath of an avalanche. What he hadn't seen was a sleigh, a reindeer or a snowman.

"Kristoff!" Bulda said, running over to him. "You're just in time! Young Pebble is missing! What if he's been hurt? What if he got lost in the woods?"

Kristoff leaned down and gave Bulda a hug. "Don't worry, Bulda. We'll find Pebble. I used to get lost in the woods, too, remember? You found me and everything turned out okay. I'm sure it will be the same with Pebble. Now, when did he go missing?"

"It was right around the time that Olaf and Sven left to –"

Kristoff nodded. "I have a good idea where little Pebble went. Don't worry, I'll have him back home very soon."

CHAPTER 13

Sure enough, Pebble was exactly where Kristoff thought he was – enjoying his time as part of the Official Substitute Arendelle Ice Master and Deliverer's team. He had already taught Olaf two new songs and shown Sven a shortcut. Pebble had a tendency to go on little adventures. (This was not the first time he had gone missing!)

By the time they arrived at their final stop before the castle, the sun was low in the sky. Candles flickered in the windows of a farmhouse, and from the barn came the low moo of a cow. It was a lovely little farm tucked into a glen right outside Arendelle.

Pulling up in front of the farmhouse, Olaf called out, "Hello!" A moment later, a grouchy-looking farmer came out on to the porch. He raised an eyebrow when he saw a snowman and a troll riding on the back of Kristoff's reindeer. "Where's Kristoff?" he asked.

As he had done before, Olaf puffed up his chest proudly. "I am Olaf," he said. "I am the Official Substitute Arendelle Ice Master and Deliverer and I will be delivering your ice today."

Sven let out a grumpy snort. Pebble gave a little shout of protest.

"Oh!" Olaf corrected himself: "I meant *we, we* are Official Substitute Arendelle Ice Masters and Deliverers."

The farmer looked at the odd trio. A reindeer, a snowman and a troll delivering ice? *I guess stranger things have happened recently,* he thought. Then he shrugged. "As long as I get my ice, I don't care who delivers it. Bring the sleigh round behind the barn and I'll help you unload." He turned to get gloves from the house but not before adding, "Just be careful. I loaded the hayloft this morning, so the ground is covered with loose hay."

"Have no fear!" Olaf replied. "We may be *substitutes*, but we are still ice *masters*. There won't be a problem."

When they pulled up in front of the barn, they saw that the farmer hadn't been joking. Hay covered every centimetre of the ground below the hayloft door. It was dry and light, the stalks catching on anything they touched. Not willing to pass up the yummy treat, Sven lowered his head for a quick bite.

"Focus, Sven!" Olaf called. "We need to finish quickly so we can surprise Kristoff!"

Sven let out an angry grumble. But he stopped snacking on the hay.

Olaf walked to the back of the sleigh. Pebble followed along, copying everything Olaf did. When Olaf cocked his head to the side, Pebble did, too.

"Let's just push the ice off the sleigh, Pebble," Olaf said. "Then the farmer can carry it to his shed. Easy, right?"

Pebble nodded. It sounded like a good plan.

Grabbing a blanket that had been bundled up in the corner of the sleigh, Olaf held it up. "I'll just put this down on the ground and that way the ice won't hit the hay." He tossed it over the side.

Together, Olaf and Pebble got behind some of the blocks of ice and pushed. Then they pushed harder. It was faster with the two of them, but still not easy. Soon enough, they were ready to push the last ice block over the edge. They pushed and pushed together. The ice block was just at the edge of the sleigh when the farmer walked out of the back of his house. Looking up, he let out a shout.

"NO!" he cried. "Stop!"

It was too late. Olaf and Pebble pushed the ice block on to the ground.

"What have you done?" the farmer shouted.

"We didn't want you to have to do all the work," Olaf explained. "Now you just have to take them to the shed."

The farmer's face was growing red. "You dropped the ice in the hay!"

Olaf cocked his head. What did the farmer mean? He had put down a blanket first. Walking to the edge of the sleigh, he looked down.

The blanket had blown a few metres forward, and the ice was now sitting on the ground right in the middle of a pile of hay. Thick stalks of dried grass covered every centimetre of the blocks.

"It's ruined!" the farmer cried. "I needed clean, fresh ice! These aren't even full blocks, they're all melted!" He sighed. "Do you have any more ice in the sleigh?"

Olaf looked behind him. They barely had any blocks of ice left – and the rest was *supposed* to go to Cook at the palace. Olaf stopped. He didn't know what to do! Cook needed them to keep her pantry cool. Plus the ice would keep her ice-cream cake birthday surprise frozen! He wanted to give Cook a great birthday gift, but he also couldn't let Kristoff down. There was only one solution.

"Well, you are in luck!" Olaf told the farmer. "I have a few blocks left and they are all yours!"

Sven looked over his shoulder. "Harrumph?"

"It will be fine!" Olaf whispered to Sven. "The castle always has extra ice. I'm just doing what Kristoff would do."

The farmer overheard him. *The snowman was just trying to help his friend,* he thought. "You all should start heading back to the castle now before it gets too dark," the farmer said.

"Okay, well, I hope to see you again very soon!" Olaf said cheerfully.

The farmer smiled in spite of himself. "Why don't you bring Kristoff along with you next time?" he suggested.

"Harrumph," Sven snorted again, as if to say, "Finally, a good plan!"

Olaf waited for the farmer to unload the last of his ice. Then, with their load completely lightened, the reindeer, the snowman and the little troll headed into town.

As they continued on their way, Olaf grinned. He couldn't wait to get home so he could tell Kristoff all about their day!

CHAPTER 14

Olaf didn't have to wait long! The Official *Full-Time* Ice Master had beaten the *Substitute* Ice Master and his team back to Arendelle. But not before stopping at the last farm on the route.

At the farm, Kristoff had found the farmer cleaning up a pile of very wet hay. The farmer told Kristoff what his substitute had done and added, "Next time you decide to take a day off, maybe you could send a different ice harvester instead of a snowman?"

Kristoff didn't bother to explain that he hadn't actually taken the day off. He also didn't bother to explain that he hadn't made Olaf his substitute ice harvester. He didn't have time for explanations.

He needed to get back to Arendelle and have a nice long talk with Olaf and Sven – and hopefully find Pebble.

After saying a hasty goodbye and apologizing yet again, Kristoff had raced down into Arendelle. He arrived, out of breath, in the stable yard. Sven and Olaf had not returned yet. So Kristoff simply waited.

A few minutes later, there was the unmistakable jingle of Sven's harness. As Kristoff watched, the reindeer pulled the sleigh into the stable yard. On his back sat Olaf – and a small runaway troll.

Spotting Kristoff, Olaf let out a happy cry. "Kristoff!" he shouted. "You're here! I can't wait to tell you all about our day. You are going to be so proud of us!"

Kristoff walked right past Olaf and headed towards Sven. He leaned down so he was face-to-face with the reindeer. "You should have known better," he said. Sven lowered his head and let out a tiny little harrumph. "We will discuss this later. I bet you had a crazy day, pal," he said, laughing gently. Then Kristoff turned back to Olaf.

The snowman had no clue how many problems he had caused during the day. Walking about, he excitedly told his version of the adventure. "As soon as I heard you tell Anna about your picnic, I decided to come to the rescue!" Olaf began. "So I went and got Sven, who of course agreed to help." Hearing this, the reindeer shook his head. Olaf ignored him and went on. "Then, after I got the sleigh hooked up, we were off. Everyone in town came out to wish us well. Kristoff, they all liked the idea of having *me* as the Official Substitute Arendelle Ice Master and Deliverer! Maybe we should talk about making the job permanent?"

The snowman's excitement was contagious and Kristoff had to hold back a smile. Instead, he raised an eyebrow.

"Okay, well, maybe not right now," said Olaf. "We can talk about it later. Anyhoo, then we went all the way up the North Mountain to your favourite ice-gathering place and collected all the blocks we needed. It was a piece of cake."

Kristoff's eyebrow rose even higher. He had seen the logs and the mess at the lake's shore. He knew it had been anything but a piece of cake.

Still, Olaf continued. "After that we went to Mr Oaken's trading post. He was so happy to see us, Kristoff! We had a teensy, tiny problem at first, but all's well that ends well! We put the ice away and then off we went. We were planning to go quickly, but then …" Olaf stopped and clapped his hands together in excitement. "Oh, Kristoff, you are going to be so happy when you hear this part! We found another lake! It is a brand-new place where you could probably get ice or have a nice snack with Sven, and it is *so* much closer and Sven was all worried about Marshmallow but I told him not to be because really the big guy is not that bad and then there was a small problem with a fire but it was a very small problem, which you shouldn't even worry about, and then …"

As Olaf continued to describe the rest of their journey in one long breath, Kristoff's eyebrow continued to rise. He knew his little friend only had good intentions, but when Olaf informed him that they had also brought a troll home to *visit*, Kristoff had to interrupt.

"Do you have any idea what you have done today?" he asked.

"We helped you, right?" Olaf replied hopefully, looking quickly at Pebble and Sven.

"Not exactly," Kristoff said. "You froze a sauna. You covered the farmer's ice in hay. You took a troll away from his mother. And then you showed up in town with no ice for the castle."

"But you and Anna … and your picnic –" Olaf began.

"I wanted to spend the day with Anna *tomorrow*!" Kristoff interrupted. "On my day off. And now I doubt I'll be able to go." Kristoff turned and began to walk away.

Hmmm, he seems kind of upset, Olaf thought. That was not the homecoming he had expected. Sure, the day hadn't gone perfectly (Olaf never had made it to the beach), but he was proud of himself for getting the job done. Yet he still wanted to make sure Kristoff and Anna got their picnic. And he needed to get the cook a birthday treat. His day wasn't done yet! He had to fix a few more teensy, tiny problems.

CHAPTER 15

Olaf plopped down on the ground. A moment later, Sven and Pebble joined him. The reindeer felt pretty awful about upsetting Kristoff – Sven knew he'd disappointed his friend. The young troll, however, didn't realize anyone was in trouble. He had loved his day of adventure!

"Hey!" Pebble said. "Can you show me the castle? I've always wanted to see the castle! Oh! Can we also say hi to Princess Anna? She is soooo pretty. And so nice."

Anna *was* nice. So was Kristoff. They deserved to have a lovely picnic together and Olaf would make that picnic happen. A picnic on a hot day … who wouldn't want that?

"Why don't you just help him out tomorrow?" Pebble suggested, putting his chubby little hands on his chubby little sides. "I'll hang out with you, Anna and Kristoff tonight and you can show me around Arendelle. Tomorrow can be Kristoff's picnic day!"

"Wait!" Olaf cried. "That's it! Pebble, you're a genius!"

The troll smiled proudly. "Really? My mum tells me I have too many ideas."

Olaf hopped up. "I have to find Kristoff!"

As Olaf began to walk away (as fast as a little snowman could walk), Sven and Pebble traded looks. Then they both shrugged and followed him.

After talking to Olaf, Kristoff had gone back to the castle. He wanted to see Anna. She always knew what to say and, right then, he needed advice. Meeting her in the courtyard, he told her about Olaf's adventures and how he'd reacted. Anna got a funny look on her face.

"He was just trying to help you, Kristoff," she said. "If I recall correctly, you tried to help me out once, too, remember? When I had to get Elsa back to Arendelle?"

Kristoff nodded.

"That turned out a little better," Anna went on, "but the point is, when someone tries to help, you shouldn't complain if it doesn't go perfectly."

Kristoff sighed. "I hope I wasn't too hard on him. Maybe I need to go talk to him again."

Luckily, Olaf was already walking into the courtyard with Sven and Pebble. "Kristoff!" he called. "There you are! I just had the greatest idea in the history of greatest ideas. I'll just help you *tomorrow*!" He looked over his shoulder. "Well, *we'll* help you. Right, guys?" Sven and Pebble nodded. "If we all work together, we can get everything done three times faster. You'll be able to deliver your ice *and* go on your picnic with Anna."

Standing next to Kristoff, Anna whispered, "Remember, if someone wants to help, that is a *good* thing."

Kristoff nodded. Turning back to Olaf, he said, "You know what? That sounds like a fantastic idea. I'm sorry I got upset earlier. You were only trying to help."

"True," Olaf said. "I probably should have checked with you first, but I love surprises!"

Kristoff started to smile, so Olaf continued. "I knew what I was doing most of the time, though. Sven and I make a great team, you know?"

Kristoff laughed. "Wanna know a secret, Olaf?"

Olaf nodded. "Yes, I love secrets!"

"When I was younger, I fell *into* the lake trying to get ice! I even ruined a brand-new pair of boots. For a long time, the other ice harvesters called me icicle, because that day I looked just like one! I didn't always know what to do, either."

Olaf laughed. At least *he* hadn't fallen into the lake. Yes, he had fallen down a hill, but that was completely different.

"So for tomorrow," Kristoff went on, "I think you should watch me and learn the right way to deliver ice. Who knows, maybe in time *you* could become the Official Arendelle Ice Master and Deliverer!"

Olaf began to bounce around happily. "That would be the greatest day ever! Well, that day and the day I finally get to go to the beach. That day would be pretty great, too. But wait! Kristoff, can you help me with something else?"

Kristoff nodded.

"Can you help me get an ice-cream cake for the cook?" asked Olaf.

"Of course," Kristoff said. "It would be my pleasure."

CHAPTER 16

So the very next morning, bright and early, Olaf and Pebble met Kristoff and Sven in the stables. This time, they had no trouble getting the harness on together. They had no trouble getting the ice out of the lake and loading it. Kristoff even taught Olaf how to cut the ice properly, which Olaf thought was tremendous fun. When they made their deliveries to Oaken, they put the ice in the right shed this time and both apologized once more. Together, they took Pebble back to his family. Then they returned to the farm, where Olaf even managed to win over the grouchy farmer, who, it turned out, couldn't resist the happy-go-lucky snowman.

Finally, they made their way back to Arendelle just in time to pick up the cake for Cook and put it in the now very full and – thanks to the new ice delivery – very cold freezer.

With everything done, it was time for Kristoff and Anna to go on their picnic.

"So, do you want to do this again tomorrow?" Olaf asked as Kristoff turned to go.

Kristoff smiled. "I don't know about tomorrow, but how about we do this once every month? And on that day every month, you won't be the Official *Substitute* Arendelle Ice Master and Deliverer, you'll be the Official *Apprentice* Ice Master and Deliverer!"

Olaf let out a little squeal of joy. "That would be perfection!" he said. True, he *might* have been on thin ice for a moment, but he had never been *too* worried. After all, Olaf knew everything would work out. Now things were better than ever.

And that seemed like a pretty good way for things to be.

THE END